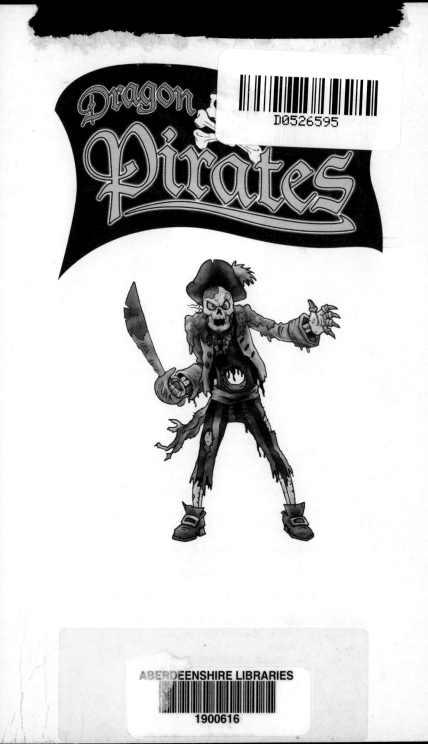

Dragon Pirates

For Rod, the navigator

JF

www.dragonbloodpirates.co.uk

First published in 2008 by Lothian Children's Books,
an imprint of Hachette Livre Australia
First published in the UK in 2010 by Orchard Books

ISBN 978 1 40830 743 4

Text © Dan Jerris 2008
Skull, crossbones and ragged parchment image © Brendon De Suza
Map illustrations on pages 4–5 © Rory Walker, 2008
Pull-out map designed by Kinart
All other illustrations © Orchard Books 2010

10 9 8 7 6 5 4 3 2 1

Printed in Great Britain by J F Print Ltd., Sparkford, Somerset

Orchard Books is a division of Hachette Children's Books,
an Hachette UK company.

www.hachette.co.uk

Dragon Blood Pirates

Skulls and Sabres

Dan Jerris

ORCHARD BOOKS

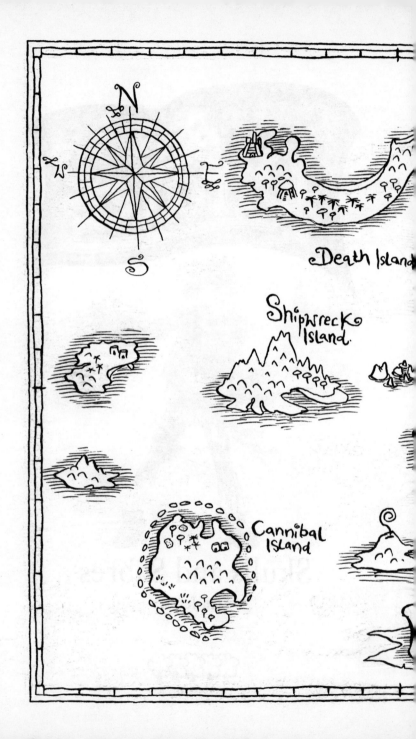

Death Island

Shipwreck Island.

Cannibal Island

Sabre Island

Town

Dragon's Stomach

Snake Island

Ghost Island

Dragon Blood Islands

Pirate Mateys and Scallywags

Alleric (Al) Breas: Lives in Drake Drive and owns a mysterious sea trunk that takes him to the Dragon Blood Islands.

Jack Seabrook: Al's best friend.

Blacktooth McGee: A very nasty pirate who runs the brigantine *The Revenge*.

Flash Johnny: Blacktooth's devious and greedy cabin boy.

Snakeboot: A magical white three-legged cat with purple eyes. Legend has it he once belonged to a terrifying pirate called Vicious Victor.

Pigface McNurt: Blacktooth's bosun; a massive pirate with a ring through his nose.

Snotty Nell: A horrible one-eyed pirate who sails a frigate called *The Tormentor*.

Grenda: Snotty Nell's daughter.

Sharkbait: Snotty Nell's one-legged bosun.

Vampire Zu: Snotty Nell's huge first mate.

Gunner: The pirate captain of the ship *The Booty*.

Mozzy: *The Booty*'s bosun (petty officer).

Slicer: *The Booty*'s cook.

Mahoot: Captain Gunner's cabin boy.

Grandfather: Mahoot's grandfather and guardian of the swimming elephants on Sabre Island.

Stanley Spong: A crooked, sneaky trader who cheats people.

Vicious Victor: A pirate ghost. He used to pillage the Dragon Blood Islands and he stole Prince Alleric's magical sabre.

Prince Alleric: The prince who once ruled Sabre Island but disappeared in mysterious circumstances.

Halimeda (Hally) Breas: Al's younger sister.

Greeny Joe: A shark so big and old that mould grows on his skin, making him glow green in the dark.

Ghost Island

Al was dreaming he was at home watching TV. The smell of a roast dinner cooking in the oven and the comfort of his couch in the lounge room made him smile. Jack, his best friend, came through the front door, sat down beside him and gave him a playful punch on the shoulder. Then he punched him harder.

Al's dream evaporated. He awoke to find Jack shaking him. It took Al a second to realise he wasn't at home but in the main cabin of the pirate ship *The Booty*, where it was dark and damp. Al's stomach rumbled. He was really hungry.

Around him the crew of *The Booty* snored, deep in sleep, exhausted after hours of bailing and fighting at sea. They had nearly sunk in a storm, but had been washed ashore on Ghost Island.

Al's sister, Hally, was sleeping heavily in the corner beside him. Snakeboot the cat was curled up beside Hally, but his ever-watchful purple eyes stared purposefully at the cabin door. He twitched his tail, fully alert.

"Jack, what are you doing?" said Al. "I was so happy sleeping."

"Listen," said Jack.

Al listened. He could hear the lap of waves on the hull and the creaking of the ship as it shifted on the sand.

"What? I can't hear anything unusual."

A sudden thump came from above. Then another. The cabin door shook and a ghostly cry raised the hair on Al's arms. "Is it a sea bird?" he asked.

"No," said Jack. His face was pale. "Someone's out there, calling for us."

The terrifying cry came again from
just outside the door. Al jumped to his
feet, opened the cabin door a crack and
peered out. The first sunrays had tinged the
morning fog red. Clouds of blood-coloured
vapour drifted around the wrecked *Booty*.
In the steaming mist Al thought he saw
a man, bent and wavering in the strange
light. Then, closer to the door, another man
turned to stare at the boys. His face was a
rotting mask, with lumps of flesh peeling
from his skull. The apparition raised a
skeletal hand and pointed. "Snakeboooot,"
he exclaimed as
he spied the three-legged cat standing at
Al's feet.

Al shut the door with a bang. "Am I still
asleep?" he cried. "Jack, pinch me!"

"Unfortunately you're awake," said Jack.
"I saw them too. I think Gunner was right.
There *are* ghosts on this island."

The boys stepped over Slicer, the cook, who was still sleeping, and went to the cabin window. The sun was cutting through the fog, revealing a skull-like rock jutting out of the sea. Lava had once flowed from the towering volcano that loomed over the island. Forbidding caverns in the rock made the eye sockets and the nose. The crooked teeth plunged into the water and waves lapped around the jaw. "It sure is a spooky-looking place," said Al. "Maybe it was just the fog playing tricks."

"The fog can't say 'Snakeboot'," said Jack.

One by one the crew woke up. Mahoot, the cabin boy, was rubbing the sleep from his eyes. Al went over to him. "Mahoot," he whispered, "are there really ghosts on this island?"

Mahoot's eyes went wide. He nodded. "Shhh," he said. "They are the ghosts of Vicious Victor's pirates. Don't mention them. Even saying the name 'Vicious Victor' is unlucky." The words had just left his mouth when footsteps thumped on the deck outside. Mahoot paled.

Slicer jumped to his feet and clutched his sword.

Mozzy, the bosun, shook Captain Gunner awake. "Captain," he squealed, "they've found us already!"

Captain Gunner sat up. He, too, heard the clumping of ghostly feet on the deck. Then a voice echoed eerily through the cabin. "Come out! Come out and join us."

All the pirates ran to the back of the cabin and cowered against the wall furthest from the door. Captain Gunner picked up a musket and pointed it at the door. "You're not gunner come in here!" he shouted.

The commotion woke Hally, who looked around in fright. "What's happening?" she asked.

"Vicious Victor's ghost crew is on board," said Captain Gunner, "and if they get to us they're gunner take our bodies."

Jack and Al looked at each other in disbelief.

"Ghosts?" Hally shrieked, bursting into tears and running to her brother's side. "Al, I want to go home *now*. I don't want to play pirates. Please, please take me home."

Al fingered the old iron key in his pocket. The rusty key unlocked the magical sea trunk back in his attic at home, at number five Drake Drive. He wished he was there right now, eating a nice roast dinner and watching TV. But he, Hally and Jack had made the decision to come to the Dragon Blood Islands to search for the Dragon Blood Sabre. There was

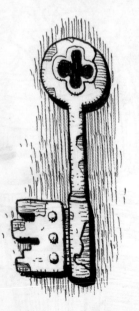

no going home unless they could find the magical portal back to the twenty-first century. Besides, it was Snakeboot who normally showed them the way home. Now the cat just sat by the cabin door while the ghosts called his name.

"I'm sorry, but I don't know how to get home, Hally," said Al, patting his sister's hand.

The Ghosts

Time passed and the tide came in, leaving a channel of water between Ghost Island and *The Booty*. Strangely, the ghost invaders no longer tapped at the cabin door or haunted the ship. But even though all was quiet, the superstitious pirates shivered in dread and the tension in the cabin mounted.

"If we stay in here we'll die of hunger," said Al. "It's either the ghosts or starvation. There's no choice. We have to go out."

Captain Gunner stared at Al. "You're not gunner go out there," he ordered.

"If you let Al and me go," reasoned Jack, "we can get food. We're kids. Ghost pirates probably wouldn't want to possess kids. We might be safe where you might not be. It's worth a try."

"And I really want to look for the sabre," added Al. "This is why we wanted you to bring us to Ghost Island. The sabre is supposed to be here."

"I'd much prefer you stayed safe," said Gunner, "but if you are fixed on the idea I can't stop you. Still, I'd feel better if we put it to the vote." All nodded in agreement. "All those in favour of the boys going out, say 'aye'."

"If *they* get possessed it might save a few of us," said one pirate from the back of the cabin.

"We're all doomed anyway," said another

one. "Probably best for them to die first."

This started a general argument and after several minutes of heated debate, the pirates voted in favour of the boys leaving the ship.

Al and Jack went to the door. "Are you going to come with us, Mahoot?" asked Jack.

Mahoot paled, then bravely stepped forward. "I'm not leaving you to go out

alone. You might need me," he answered.
"Besides, I want the famous sabre returned
to Sabre Island too."

"I'm coming as well," said Hally. "I don't
think a pirate ghost would want me. I can't
imagine a pirate wanting to be a little girl."

"Blinkin' barnacles, no!" agreed the
pirates in the cabin.

Snakeboot was the first to bound through

the open cabin door, followed by Jack, Al, Hally and Mahoot. The door shut with a bang behind them. Fearfully, they peered around the decks. The ghosts were nowhere to be seen. "Do you think the high tide's keeping them away?" asked Jack.

"Pirates can't swim, so you might be right," replied Al. "Even so, we'll try our luck ashore."

They lowered themselves overboard on ropes and waded through the shallow waters to the beach. Al held Snakeboot high so he wouldn't get wet. As soon as Snakeboot's paws touched the sand, he took off down the beach away from the skull rock. The volcano rumbled ominously and the island shook. The hilly sand dunes behind the beach hissed menacingly as grains of sand slid down their steep slopes.

The cat headed straight for a ruined castle a few hundred metres back from the sea.

The volcano grumbled again and spat fire into the sky. Smoking stones rained down. Al hurried his friends towards the castle ruins, hoping for cover.

The castle's gigantic wooden doors hung from their hinges. Fleeing from the dangerous rain, Snakeboot ran through the gateway into a large room. He disappeared down a flight of stairs and the children raced after him. In the bowels of the ruined building, Snakeboot moved with steady determination. He led them through a maze of rooms and corridors, dodging the fallen timbers and bricks blocking their way. Al reasoned that Snakeboot had always led them to safety; he had even found treasure for them. He hoped that this time the cat wasn't going to lead them into danger.

The building shook from another earth tremor. Dust showered down and the air became stale and musty. Snakeboot continued down a long passageway, which ended abruptly outside an iron door blocked by fallen roof beams. The cat pawed at the door.

"Are you trying to show me where the sabre is?" asked Al, patting the cat.

Snakeboot miaowed in response, so Al pulled at the door.

"There's no way we can get in there," said

Mahoot. "It's jammed by those timbers."

Al picked up Snakeboot. "Sorry, old puss, but you've led us to a dead end. We're going back."

As they retraced their steps, several glowing shapes scuttled into the shadows. Unearthly eyes followed their every move. More gruesome ghouls gathered at the end of the hall, forcing them to stop. The ghostly horde crept closer, eyeing them maliciously. They all stepped back.

"Maybe it's daylight that keeps them away," said Jack. "It's pretty dark in here." He pulled out the sword he'd found on Cannibal Island and waved it angrily at the ghosts.

"I don't think waving a sword will help," whispered Al. "They are already dead."

Nonetheless, the ghosts fell back at the sight of the sword, then rallied and shuffled forward once again. Al, Jack, Mahoot and

Hally all moved back until they found themselves at the blocked iron door with nowhere to go.

Al faced the ghosts. "Let us pass," he said.

"We will get you eventually," moaned a rotting man. The ghosts came so close they could almost touch the children.

Suddenly, the ground shook violently and part of the ceiling above the creatures collapsed. The ghosts moved back slightly and Al looked around desperately for a way of escape. The earth shook again, this time knocking the children off their feet. The beams lying against the door behind them fell to the ground with a crash.

Choking on the dust, Jack, Al, Hally and Mahoot picked themselves up and stepped back against the door. When one of the ghosts moved nearer, Jack held his sword high in defence. The reeking ghoul hesitated and groaned. With the door now

unblocked, Al turned
and pulled at the its
handle. The door
opened a crack
and Snakeboot
rushed through.
With a squeak the
door opened alittle
more, just wide
enough for Hally
to squeeze inside.
Then Al stood
guard as Mahoot
and Jack wedged
themselves in. Just
as another ghost
reached out to grab
him, Al forced
himself through the
gap. Then together
Al and Jack slammed

the iron door shut, while the pirate ghosts howled on the other side.

"They aren't coming through," said Al, relieved. "Like on *The Booty*, they're staying on the other side of the door. I wonder why..."

"You're right, for some reason they're not floating through the walls," said Jack, "but we don't want them sliding through a crack." He pressed his body hard against the door. Al and Mahoot also leant against it in case the ghosts found a way through.

"We can't stay like this forever," declared Mahoot.

"The door has a lock and a keyhole," said Jack, "but there's no key."

Al remembered the key he kept in his pocket. He pulled it out and pushed it into the lock. The key turned and the door was locked safely against the ghosts.

"We're safe!" cried Mahoot.

They found themselves in a large room. A small barred window let in some light. Boxes and chests were piled high against the walls and some stray jewels and doubloons glinted in the dust on the floor.

"We're safe for the moment," said Al, "but I think we're stuck in Vicious Victor's old treasure room. This is worse than being stuck on *The Booty*." He looked at Snakeboot. "What were you thinking, leading us here?"

In answer the cat rolled on his back and purred, showing his tummy. Then he mewed again and again as if he were calling somebody.

"There's a terrible smell in here," said Hally, sniffing and screwing up her face.

Al sniffed the air too. "It smells like rotting meat."

"It's getting stronger," said Jack, holding his nose.

To their horror, a shimmering, skeletal
man wearing a gold frockcoat appeared at
the back of the room. His long lank beard,
decorated with red ribbons, hung from his
jaw bone. For a few frightening seconds,
the shadowy creature floated just above the
floor of the treasure room. Slowly he came
closer, rotting and horrible.

He tipped his head back and, with a
bloodcurdling cackle, moved towards them.
Mahoot and Jack leapt back against the door.
Hally whimpered and shut her eyes.

"Keep away!" Al croaked, terrified by the
ghost. "Stand back, Vicious Victor!" Despite
his fear and the thump of his heart, Al
stepped forward to meet the hideous creature.

The ghost laughed again and, ignoring Al, he bent down and reached out with his bony, bejewelled hands, crying, "*There* you are! You've been gone a long time. Come, come."

Snakeboot's purrs of joy echoed around the treasure room as he bounded to the ghost's feet. The frightful ghoul picked him up and cradled him in his arms. "So, who have you brought me?" he asked, as his dreadful eyes fell upon them.

Vicious Victor's Story

Hally, Mahoot, Jack and Al all huddled by the door, too afraid to speak. The ghost of Vicious Victor stared at them for a few minutes, then asked, "You know who I am, but I would like to know who has come to visit me."

"I'm Al Breas," Al replied, his voice quavering. "I'm with my sister, Hally, and my best friends, Jack and Mahoot."

"And why are you here? You are obviously

brave or you wouldn't have got this far."

"Snakeboot brought us here," said Al.

"If he did," said Vicious Victor, "then you must want something."

"We read Prince Alleric's diary," said Al, "and it told us to go to Ghost Island to search for the Dragon Blood Sabre."

"Just a minute...Al and Hally? It wouldn't be Alleric and Halimeda, would it?" asked the ghost. "Are they your names?"

Al nodded. "And Breas, is that your last name?" Al nodded again. "If you rearrange it, it would spell Sabre. You must be a grandchild of

Sabre Island. I have your sabre here. I have waited many a long year to return it."

"Why do you want to return it?" asked Jack, recovering slightly from the shock of finding himself face to face with Vicious Victor's ghost.

"I must return everything I stole," the ghost sighed sadly. "This is the curse of Ghost Island." His body slumped and he looked miserable.

"How did you get in here?" asked Hally.

Vicious Victor stared at Hally for several seconds, then said, "I will answer your question, but it will take time to tell my terrible tale." He gestured to the side of the room. "If I were you, I'd take a box and sit on it. Make yourself comfortable."

Al pulled out a small treasure chest and sat down. The others did the same.

Vicious Victor began his story. He explained how he had become the most feared pirate in all of the Dragon Blood Islands because of his murderous pillaging. He had so much plunder he had to store it somewhere. He had heard of Ghost Island and, knowing it was feared by everyone, he decided to build his castle here. No one would ever come looking for him on an island with such a terrible curse attached to it.

But no matter how rich and safe Victor was, he was still greedy and jealous. Only Prince Alleric was richer than him, and all because he was lucky enough to own magical jewels and the legendary sabre. So Victor plotted to raid the prince's castle, kill him, and take his treasure. He especially wanted the sabre because it would take him through time and space and allow him to steal where and when he wanted.

One night Victor sailed to Sabre Island, but Prince Alleric was away. Only his sister, Halimeda, and the servants were in the castle. Victor raided Alleric Castle and took the sabre from the princess, along with loads of treasure.

However, on the way back to Ghost Island, the weather turned foul. Great storms beset his feared ship, *The Nemesis*, and it began to sink from the weight of the treasure on board. As storm after storm battered his ship, Victor was forced to

lighten its load by burying the treasure on different islands, until he eventually made it back to his secret hideaway on Ghost Island.

Then he discovered that the sabre wouldn't work for him. No matter what he tried, it would not take him anywhere. He realised that only Prince Alleric knew how to use the ancient magic. He decided to capture the prince and force him to reveal the magic words.

Victor left clues here and there about the location of the sabre so Prince Alleric would find them and come to Ghost Island.

One night, while the volcano was erupting, Prince Alleric sailed into the bay. Great stones fell upon the castle and smashed down the doors. The earthquake was so violent that Vicious Victor didn't capture Prince Alleric as planned. Instead he faced the heroic prince in fearful hand-to-hand combat.

"As the earth shook and knocked me

off my feet," continued Vicious Victor, "the prince – your grandfather – grabbed the sabre from my hands. He staggered away, cut and bleeding from our fight. The volcano erupted and I took after him with my men. We couldn't let him get very far in case he said the magical words and disappeared with the sabre.

"Lava from the volcano flowed into the sea and a great hissing fog surrounded us. My men and I forced your grandfather to my locked treasure room. With his back to the door, he found the key I had unfortunately left hanging from a hook on the wall. He opened the door, leapt inside, and locked it behind him. I had a spare key around my neck so I opened the door, but it was too late! When I got in there, Prince Alleric was holding his sabre high, shimmering with a golden light. I hadn't heard the magic words. Angrily, I leapt and grabbed the sabre from his hands just as he vanished.

"I had the sabre once again, but Prince Alleric was gone. Then the volcano gave a mighty roar. The earth shook and my castle collapsed. I was trapped. I survived for days, surrounded by my gold, until I,

too, faded away. My crew were killed in the earthquake, all except Snakeboot and my first mate."

"Why don't you just go out and give it all back?" asked Hally.

"I can't do that," replied Victor. "My sins were so awful that the island won't release me."

"Do the other pirate ghosts really steal bodies?" asked Al. "Are you going to steal our bodies now?"

"No," said Victor. "I have learnt my lesson. I can fix my bad deeds from here, thanks to this cat.

"Snakeboot grew older and older – he's more than a hundred years old. I believe the island has given him strange powers. He isn't cursed to remain on the island, as he isn't bad. The other pirates are searching for bodies to steal so they can go on being evil. They refuse to listen and understand that if they go on doing bad things, they will return here again and again. There is no escape from Ghost Island for the wicked."

"Why didn't Snakeboot find Prince Alleric then?" asked Al.

"He searched," said Victor. "He went everywhere, even back to Sabre Island, but your grandfather had vanished."

"He must've gone forward in time," said Jack. "We come from hundreds of years into the future, and Al's grandfather only died about six years ago. He left a magical sea trunk in the attic. It brought us here, to the Dragon Blood Islands."

"That explains it then," said Victor. "Sabre Island was once the home of mighty magicians and your grandfather inherited many of their magical charms. He was always a lucky one – I was jealous of him."

"How did Snakeboot find us when we first arrived?" asked Al. "We were on a rock in the middle of the ocean... And how does he know how to take us home?"

"That's the wonderful thing about having these strange gifts," said Victor. "Snakeboot is very good at finding the people I robbed. He has an animal's instinct and other magic that can't be explained, and he helps me to right all the wrongs I did." Victor hugged his cat lovingly. "He is the most wonderful creature."

"He sure is," piped in Hally. "I called him Furgus when I first saw him. He sleeps in my bed at home and we're good friends."

"He would have found that a very unusual experience!" said the pirate. He turned to Al and pointed to a pile of boxes. "So, grandchildren of the sabre, go over there and collect what is yours."

Al found the glorious sabre inside a wooden box. The hilt was carved with a gold dragon's head, and the mighty Dragon Blood Ruby glittered with a fiery light. Al held up the sabre. It tingled in his hand. "Where is the Scabbard of Invincibility?" he asked.

"Scabbard?" asked Victor. He scratched his beard while he thought for a moment. "There *was* a scabbard. Why was it called the Scabbard of Invincibility?"

"Whoever wore the scabbard could not be harmed by any weapon," said Jack. "The four black diamonds on it had magical powers of protection."

"How silly of me," said Victor. "I didn't realise. I ripped the diamonds off and used them to bribe four pirates I knew, who sailed other ships. If I had known the scabbard had those powers I would have worn it myself.

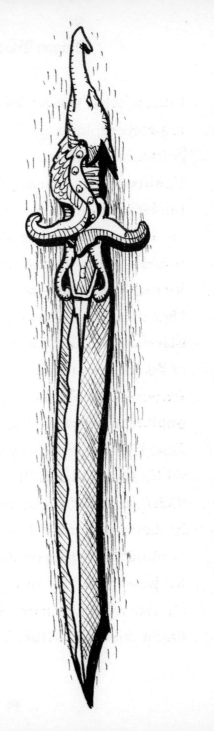

I threw what was left of it over there somewhere, long ago." He pointed to a corner of the room.

Al began to search. "What I don't understand is who left the codes and messages on the other islands."

"My first mate was still alive," answered Victor, "and heard me bewailing my fate. He escaped from the other ghosts on the island and, in fear for his soul, spent the rest of his life leaving clues for Prince Alleric's ancestors, should they ever appear, so they might find what we buried or stole."

Jack held out the old sword he'd found on Cannibal Island. "I think this is yours, then," he said. "I found it near a skeleton."

Victor inspected the rusty old weapon. "I must have dropped it after I buried some treasure there," he said. "Very nice of you to offer it back to me, but you can keep it. It might come in useful."

Al lifted a box away from the wall and found a dusty silver scabbard lying on the floor. "Found it!" he cried, holding the scabbard up for everyone to see.

He buckled it around his waist and placed the Dragon Blood Sabre securely inside.

"May your sabre bring you good luck," said Vicious Victor. "I hope you can find the black diamonds for the scabbard and discover the magic words to make the sabre work again."

The Ghost Ship

"It's time for you to go,' said Victor, signalling for them to open the locked door.

"How will we get out of your castle?" asked Al. "Those men of yours are intent on hurting us."

Victor held out his skeletal hands. "These rings will keep you safe," he said. "My men will know you're under my protection." He pulled a golden ring from his index finger. It was a dragon coiled in a circle with its head biting its tail. Glowing rubies shone in its eyes. "I stole this from Alleric Castle," Victor explained, "and so it is yours by right." He handed the ring to Al.

The next ring he removed was from his little finger. "This one I took from Princess Halimeda when I stole the sabre. She was very brave, trying to protect her brother's treasures, so we didn't kill her." He held out a silver dragonhead ring with a pearl set in the dragon's mouth. It fitted neatly onto Hally's thumb.

He took two more rings from his hands. One was an iron ring fashioned into an elephant's head. The tusks jutted out, making it a dangerous weapon. He looked at Mahoot. "This one's yours," he said. "I took it many years ago from one of the servants at the castle."

Then his eyes fell on Jack. "And as you are a best friend, I will give you the best ring. I took this from a king. He was handsome and rich, but I burnt his town and sold him as a slave. For that crime I still suffer." He held out a thick gold ring with a star setting. In the middle of the star was a diamond and on each of the five points of the star glittered brilliant sapphires. "One day you may find the owner of this ring. Until then, wear it with pride."

They all inspected their gifts with awe. "Now go," ordered Victor. "Open the door with the key your grandfather took from this very castle."

Al put the key back into the lock and opened the iron door. He stepped out with his hand held high. The ghostly pirate crew moved away from the door at the sight of the famed ring. Jack went out next.

"Is Furgus – I mean, Snakeboot – coming with us?" asked Hally. "I know he's your cat, but I really love him."

"I care for him too," said the doomed pirate, "but I know you will need him when you hunt for the scabbard's black diamonds. I will let Snakeboot join you, but only when you come to the Dragon Blood Islands. He can stay with me when you return to your own time."

"That's fair," said Hally, and Victor gave her a strange, lipless grin. He put Snakeboot down and the cat ran to Hally.

With their new rings held high, Hally and Mahoot left the treasure room. The hideous ghosts moved back and let the children pass. They followed, shadowing them, wailing in disappointment as the four made their way out of the forbidding ruins.

As they passed through the castle gate, the volcano let out a massive rumble, followed by a mighty jolt. They ran towards the beach as the ground shook again. Behind them the castle creaked and groaned as its walls collapsed.

With the earth trembling, a towering sand dune beside them began to collapse. The mountain of sand hissed around them, knocking them flying and almost burying them alive.

Al pulled himself from the sand, grabbed Mahoot's hand and hauled him out. Hally was buried to the neck and Jack was trapped too. Mahoot and Al dug furiously with their hands to free them.

As they dusted themselves down, Al noticed a ship's mast sticking out of the sand just in front of them. The earth still trembled and shook and sand cascaded away down towards the beach, until a large black ship was revealed. Its twin masts gleamed in the smoky light of the volcano and a breeze rustled the ancient canvas of the sails. The children shivered.

"It's *The Nemesis*," said Al. "And it's perfectly preserved."

"It looks very spooky," said Jack.

"How do you think it got way up here, metres away from the beach?" asked Mahoot.

"Maybe the pirates dragged it here," suggested Hally.

"Something must have," said Al as he looked towards the ocean. "It sure is a long way from the beach."

"That's odd," said Jack, "the tide's way, way, way out. *The Booty*'s high and dry, and the tide's still going out. Look, there's even a fish flopping on the sand."

Jack's words rang warning bells. If what Al was thinking was right, then he only had a few minutes to try to save everyone's lives.

"Stay here!" he shouted. "Climb aboard *The Nemesis* and don't leave it for any reason. I have to run to *The Booty*!" Leaving his friends open-mouthed and confused, Al took to his heels and tore down the beach.

"We should do what he says," Jack

called out. "The sand still holds the ship on one side, so let's climb up there and get on board." He picked up Snakeboot and the three of them set off to explore the ghostly ship.

Al raced the last few metres to the wrecked *Booty*. "Gunner!" he screamed with all his might. "Get off *The Booty* now! If you don't abandon ship, you'll be killed!"

Whether it was the urgency in Al's voice, or the fact that the pirates could no longer stand being confined below decks, Gunner and the crew scrambled outside. The captain leant over the rail. "What's going on?" he called down to Al.

"Tsunami!"

Gunner and his crew stared back at him blankly.

"Tidal wave!" screamed Al. "Follow me! Run for your lives!"

The pirates needed no further prompting. They leapt from the stricken *Booty* and ran after Al as he raced up the beach towards *The Nemesis*.

As the pirates climbed aboard, Al turned and looked back. Far out to sea a dark line fringed with white foam loomed on the horizon. As a strange stillness came over the island, a sea bird cried a warning. Al wasted no time. He ran up the sand bank and slid

down onto the deck with only seconds
to spare.

The huge wave roared towards the shore.
An enormous wall of water smashed onto
the beach and pulverised *The Booty*. The
tidal wave swirled towards *The Nemesis*,
picked it up and spun it around. The ship
rocked crazily then see-sawed, spilling
everyone across the decks. The timbers
groaned and the ancient sails flapped
thunderously. Then the vast wall of water
retreated and sucked *The Nemesis* out to sea.

Possessed

Once *The Nemesis* was stable, Gunner took charge and the crew set to work, clearing the decks and trimming the sails. A fair breeze blew from the south and they set a course for one of the outer islands.

When all had settled, Gunner rubbed his hands with glee. "*The Nemesis* is mine," he cried, "and never a finer ship sailed the seas!"

Slicer strutted down the deck waving a knife. "We can go raiding and no one can catch us," he said. "Who will we attack first?"

Mozzy came up beside Gunner. "You know, Captain," he sneered, "we should gun down the first ship we see and take everyone on board as slaves. We need people to build us a fort."

Gunner's eyes glinted with fire at the suggestion. "I was going to say we should head for the nearest island and plunder the first village we come across," he roared.

Al looked at Jack, confused. "Captain Gunner," he said, "perhaps we should go to town and buy supplies. There's no food on board."

"Shut up, boy," Gunner spat. "If it weren't for that ring you're wearing, I'd have you walking the plank."

Slicer pushed Jack so hard that he stumbled. "Get to work, you layabouts," he yelled, "or I'll have the cat-o-nine-tails on you."

Al grabbed Hally by the hand and, together with Mahoot and Jack, went below decks.

Al took his friends to one side. "I think we have a problem," he whispered.

"I know what you mean," said Jack. "That's not our Captain Gunner talking."

"It's the ghosts," said Mahoot, shivering.

"What can we do?" asked Hally. "I don't want to be on a ship full of bad men."

"They won't touch us," said Mahoot, rubbing his new elephant ring nervously.

"There must be a way to stop the ghosts," said Al. "Keep your eyes open and watch for a clue to saving Gunner and his crew."

Night came and Snakeboot led the children to a hide out near the gunpowder hold, far away from the troublesome ghostly crew manning the ship. Al didn't sleep well, and late into the night he woke. The creaking wood and the gentle flap of the sails told him they had a following sea and a calm night. He decided to get up, take a walk around the ship and see what was going on.

Al poked his head into the great cabin and found Gunner, Slicer, Mozzy and the crew fast asleep on the floor. He tiptoed up to Gunner and shook him. Gunner didn't move. Al pushed him and pinched the skin on the back of his hand, but he didn't even flinch. It was as if he were in some sort of coma. Puzzled, Al left him and made his way back onto the deck. He climbed onto the forecastle. Above, the stars glittered and the moon shone through clouds that scudded across the sky. On the deck, other ghostly forms were glowing an eerie green.

When the moon disappeared behind a cloud, the deathly creatures' glow grew brighter and they took on a creepy human outline. They paced the decks with contorted steps, their rotting skin squeezed over their bones, and their hair hanging grotesquely from their partially exposed skulls. The ship wallowed, unmanned and unsupervised.

Al shuddered in revulsion, but he quickly grasped that the ghosts had left his pirate friends in a death-like coma while they

wandered the decks of *The Nemesis* at night. "There has to be a way to stop them coming back to Gunner's crew in the morning," thought Al as he turned away from the dreadful apparitions and returned to his hiding place in horror.

Saving the Pirates

The next day, while the pirates were up and about, the children stayed in the hide out Snakeboot had found for them. Once he felt they were safe, Al whispered, "I've got some news. Last night, I discovered that the ghosts leave the bodies of Gunner's crew and walk the decks. They wander around the ship but they don't sail it. If we can think of a way to stop them returning in the morning light, we might be able to save our friends."

"I've been thinking too," said Jack. "Remember how we wondered what was stopping the ghosts coming into the cabin while we were on *The Booty*?"

"You thought it might be the tide or the daylight," said Hally.

"Yes, but I was wrong both times. It has to be something else that keeps them away," said Jack.

"Go back to the beginning," said Al. "Why didn't they come through the door when we first landed on Ghost Island?"

"Perhaps it was the hinges, the nails and the iron bands that held the wood onto the door," suggested Mahoot. "Grandfather always keeps an iron bar in our house to protect us from evil spirits."

"It's true," said Jack. "My mum has the same superstition. We have a horseshoe by the door made of iron. Mum says it's for luck."

"You're right," said Al. "I've noticed that

every doorway is left open on this ship."

"But what stopped them getting to us when we walked to Vicious Victor's fort and through the passageways?" asked Jack.

"If it's iron, I have an iron key in my pocket and, Jack, you had that rusty old sword," replied Al. "And now that I think about it, the ghosts fell back when you waved your sword at them."

Hally touched her hair. "I had hairpins. I think they're made of iron, because they get rusty if I leave them in the bathroom."

"See a pin and pick it up, all day long you'll have good luck," chimed Mahoot.

"So we were protected before we got into the treasure room," said Al, "and it had an iron door, which stopped them coming through. If we're right, then we can protect Gunner and the crew. We'll put something made of iron on each one of our friends while the ghosts wander around the decks at night."

They were interrupted as the ship suddenly headed up into the wind, and the pulleys and winches began to grind as the sails were pulled down.

Jack went out to the nearest porthole and came back to report that an island lay off to starboard. Within minutes the rattle of the anchor and the lowering of the ropes to the longboat told the children that the ghostly pirates were planning to row ashore.

"Did you see a town?" asked Al.

"No, it's just a small island, but there's a river flowing out to sea and a small lagoon," said Jack.

"They'll be taking on water, I should think," said Mahoot.

While the pirate crew ferried water onto *The Nemesis*, the children searched the ship for anything made of iron: iron nails, an old iron pot in the galley, a knife with a rusty blade and some old tools, until they had several bags full of what they hoped would save their friends.

After the pirates had returned and were busy working, Al and Jack sneaked onto the deck and placed various objects centimetres apart around the entire ship. Then they went below.

As the sun was setting the children crept into the great cabin with as much iron as they could carry, then hid themselves and waited.

Just after sunset, Gunner and his men marched into the great cabin, lined up in a row and suddenly tumbled to the ground like dead men. Seconds later, the evil ghouls flickered up from the pirates' comatose bodies, swirled into the air, laughed, and floated out of the room.

As soon as the ghosts were up on deck, the children set to work, placing a piece of iron on each unconscious man. Then, taking it in turns to stay awake, they stood guard over their friends so nothing would move the items from their bodies.

Just before sunrise the children hid themselves once again.

Within minutes the ghosts shimmered slowly into the room, one by one. As each creature came to the body of a sleeping man, it stopped, agitated. Then it circled. As the dreadful ghouls realised they couldn't possess the bodies, they howled in surprise and displeasure. Their bloodcurdling screeches pierced the atmosphere.

To further the horror, the ghosts glowed brightly with anger. Hot green phosphorous

light filled the orbs of their eyes. The irate
creatures circled the room, searching for
victims. Ducking down, the children made
themselves as small as possible as the ghosts
came terrifyingly close.

The ghouls stayed in the great cabin until
the first rays of the sun drifted through the
portholes. Finally one of them cried, "It's

those children. They've stopped us!"

"We can't take their bodies until the iron is removed!" howled another in anguish. "How can we sail *The Nemesis* without the bodies?"

"Find them," cried another voice. "Find those disgusting children and wait for them to make a mistake!" Glowing with anger and frustration, the hideous creatures flew out of the cabin.

The children shut the door behind the ghosts, then piled iron against it. "That should stop them for a while," said Al.

They waited fearfully for the pirates to awaken. Late in the morning, they were rewarded as Slicer, who was always the first to wake, moved and sat up. Al rushed over to him. "Slicer," he whispered, "is it you?"

"Of course it's me," said Slicer. "What's wrong with you lot, you look like you've seen a ghost!"

One by one all the pirates woke up, and Al explained their plan to escape from Vicious Victor's ghost crew.

Very soon, Gunner and his men lined up at the great cabin door. Each man held onto his piece of iron tightly. Hally clutched Snakeboot to her chest, then they all moved cautiously onto the deck. Gunner's crew went to work and set the sails on the moored ship. The mighty sails flapped in the breeze and the ship swung on its anchor.

Al moved quickly to the bow of *The Nemesis* and undid the windlass key that held the anchor line fast. Then he ran to the

longboat, everyone climbed aboard, and the men cast off and lowered it to the lapping waves.

Al sighed with relief as the wind filled the sails of *The Nemesis* and it sailed, unmanned, out to sea.

"We're saved!" cried Gunner. "It may be a small island, but we are free of the ghosts!" He beamed at the children. "We have so much to thank you for. I'm gunner hold a party as soon as we hit the beach."

They all beamed back.

The Party

After they pulled the longboat onto the
beach, the pirates turned it over so it became
a shelter. The iron implements the children
had given each pirate quickly became very
useful. The men set to work. Some gathered
palm fronds and made a roof beside the
longboat to keep out the sun. Others cut
wood and, with a flint, a fire was soon
burning on the beach. The old iron pot was
filled with various fruits and vegetables and,

in typical pirate
fashion, shellfish,
a few big white
grubs and some
beach worms. Soon
a strange stew was
brewing for dinner.
No one had eaten in
days and the smell was mouth-watering.

As the sun went down everyone had a full stomach and there were smiles all round. "I never thought I'd be happy marooned on an island," said Gunner. "And I promised you a party, so we will have one." He signalled for Slicer to stand.

Slicer jumped to his feet and started clapping his hands. Other men drummed on their thighs, while another took out an old comb from his pocket and made a trumpet sound with it. Another pulled a leaf from a tree and made a whistle. Within minutes there was a band. Several pirates began to sing a sea shanty:

"The blood of a dragon flows in our veins,
And diamonds and rubies and our
ill-gotten gains.
Treasure and gold and faraway places,
Loads of wild storms and our mates'
ugly faces.
Wind in the sails and a following breeze,
These are the things that a pirate
crew needs!"

Some of the pirates danced the hornpipe and others did a jig. Hally jumped up and showed them how to be a popstar by singing her favourite songs. The pirates clapped mightily. Al pulled the magical sabre from its scabbard and sang a song of his own:

"We followed old Snakeboot around
And thanks to him the sabre is found.
To Sabre Island we're homeward bound!"

The pirates cheered. Then Jack showed everyone how to moonwalk while Al did a bit of break-dancing.

Finally, they all fell asleep, the deep, quiet sleep that comes with happiness.

The following day, everyone went foraging again. They discovered that finding food on a small island isn't an easy task. Although there was food to eat, it was running out quickly. After only one day, the fruit was almost gone and the seafood was harder to find. Snakeboot caught a snake, but no one wanted him to add it to the pot.

On the second day, Al found some oysters on the rocks. He'd never eaten an oyster before, but he'd heard they were delicious. He prised one open. It looked horrible. "It's like a big grey bogey," said Jack, peering over his shoulder. "Are you really going to eat it?"

Al didn't answer. He sliced under it and,

as he'd seen in the movies, he tipped the shell up and let the gloopy body slide into his mouth. He bit down. Something hard crunched under his teeth. He spat the oyster out and in his hand was a large silver pearl.

"Pearls!" cried Jack. "Hey, there're pearls here!"

Soon the pirates were feasting and gathering pearls. By the end of the day, they had a small collection of treasure.

"There's enough here to buy us a new ship," said Captain Gunner. "Only problem is, we don't really know where we are. It could be a long row to nowhere if we leave."

"I think we should try," said Slicer. "We can't survive here for much longer; our food will run out in a few days. It's best we go while we're fit and strong."

"We'll put it to the vote," said Gunner.

All the pirates agreed that they should set out to sea. "Make a mast," ordered Gunner, "and we'll take off our shirts and make a sail. Then we'll head south. And by hook or by crook, we're gunner make town in no time flat."

The New Ship

A few days later the longboat was still far from land. There had been a strong breeze, but now there was not a puff of wind. The sun beat down and the pirates who were rowing stopped for a break. They rubbed their tired and blistered hands. Hunger gnawed once again at Al's stomach, and Hally's lips were dry and cracked from lack of water.

Jack eyed the sea water thirstily.

"Don't drink it," warned Mahoot. "You must never drink sea water because it makes you go mad and jump overboard."

As if to remind everyone of that dreadful fate, a large green fin cut the water nearby. Greeny Joe, the most feared shark in the Dragon Blood Islands, had found them, and was now circling the ship.

"Are we going to die?" whispered Hally.

Al couldn't answer her. He looked away from his sister's face. "Don't cry," he said. "It'll waste water."

That night a shower of rain provided them with drinking water. It also brought a fresh breeze and the shirt sail pushed the tired pirates further south. As dusk fell, some flying fish were disturbed by the ship and flew into the air. Their shining wings whirred overhead. Snakeboot leapt high, his front paws hooking down onto the floor of the longboat. Then he leapt again.

Within minutes their amazing cat had
pulled down about twenty fish. Jack used his
sword to cut them up and everyone sucked
at the raw flesh. This was enough to give
them strength.

The following day, they caught sight of
land. The men rowed with gusto towards it.
Eventually they found themselves at a small

village. Gunner paid a boatman one pearl for food and water, and to sail them into the main town and port of the Dragon Blood Islands.

Another pearl bought them all much-needed beds for the night in a small hotel. Early the next morning they followed Gunner to the docks to look for boats.

It didn't take long for Gunner to spy a battered old galleon. She had three masts and nine sails. There was some cannon damage to her top deck and towering stern-castle, but otherwise she was sea worthy. The old galleon's name-plate had been destroyed in battle and on her prow was the figurehead of a black lion rearing up to face the waves. "She's a dandy of a ship," said Gunner as he strode across her decks.

"She's a real dandy," agreed Slicer. "And she's as sound as can be."

Gunner counted out the pearls to the old owner and the galleon was his.

"We have enough money left for provisions and to fix her up," Gunner said gleefully, as he stood with his hands on his hips admiring his new possession.

"What will you call her?" asked Jack.

"The Dandy-lion?" quipped Al.

Gunner clapped his hands. "That's

clever," he said. "Yes, I'm gunner call her *The Dandylion*!"

While the pirates were admiring their new ship, Snakeboot pawed at Al's leg. "Not now, Snakeboot. We've got work to do. We've got to take the sabre back to Sabre Island and find out how it works."

Snakeboot, however, was not put off, and continued to claw at Al's leg. When he finally had Al's attention, he moved off down the road away from the port.

"Snakeboot wants us to follow," Al whispered to Jack. He grabbed his sister's hand and they followed their cat.

Snakeboot took them down some familiar streets to an old warehouse. He pawed at a locked door, which Al opened with the key he had in his pocket. "It's time to go home, Hally," he said. "Snakeboot wants us to go home now."

"Goodbye, Furgus," said Hally, and she

gave the cat a hug. Snakeboot reached up
with a paw and hooked the hem of her long
dress. "I mean, Snakeboot." Hally popped
a kiss onto her finger and touched the cat's
nose in farewell.

"We'll come back and visit, I promise,"
said Al.

As soon as they stepped inside the
warehouse, they felt the familiar tingle in their
arms and legs, which told them they were

travelling back to the twenty-first century.

Seconds later they found themselves in Al's attic at number five Drake Drive. A scrumptious roast-dinner aroma wafted through the house. Al's dad's voice floated up to them. "Come on, you kids! Dinner!"

"Can Jack stay?" Al yelled back.

"Go and ring his mum," called his dad.

They peeled out of their pirate clothes and put them in the cupboard, ready to be worn again. Al carefully placed the sabre and the scabbard inside the magical sea trunk, which he locked with the iron key. "You should be safe in here till I can take you back to Alleric Castle," he whispered. Then he raced to the bathroom to wash his hands before dinner.

They sat down at the table as Al's dad brought in the food. "I've never been so hungry in my life," said Jack, devouring the food.

"You kids played well together today," said Dad. "It's great to see you getting on so well."

"Hally makes a good pirate," said Jack.

"This is the most delicious dinner I've ever eaten," said Hally, poking a huge forkful of roast potatoes into her mouth.

"Where's Furgus?" asked Dad.

"Oh, we found his owner," replied Al.

He winked at Hally. Later, Jack and Al watched TV together. "You know," said Jack, "I'm looking forward to going back to the Dragon Blood Islands and finding out more about the magical sabre."

"Me too," said Al. "It's much better than watching TV."

Jack gave his friend a playful punch on the shoulder, then said, "It's like a really good dream, isn't it?"

Al had to agree.

Arrr! Ahoy there, mateys!

hoist the sails and drop the anchor: ye have some treasure to find!

One swashbucklin' reader will win a haul of booty, including an Xbox console and games and an iTunes voucher, and twelve runners up will win a Dragon Blood Pirates booty bag.

For a chance to win, ye must dare to unearth the treasure using the Dragon Blood Islands map from *Death Diamond* (also available to download at www.dragonbloodpirates.co.uk), and the six big pirate stickers that are inserted in every book.

Each of the six Dragon Blood Pirates books contains a clue revealing an island protected by a dastardly pirate, and a sticker of the pirate to place on your map. When ye have solved the six clues, and have placed the six stickers, there will remain only one island, where the pirate booty be.

To win, enter online at
www.dragonbloodpirates.co.uk

Or send your name, address and the name of the island where the treasure lies to:

Dragon Blood Pirates Treasure Hunt
338 Euston Road, London NW1 3BH

Best o' luck, me hearties!

To find where the pirate sticker
from *Skulls and Sabres* should go,
ye must find the answer to
the clue that lies below:

The island on which this ghostly pirate roams Is where you will find pirate shops and pirate homes.

If you get stuck, fear not, for there be
extra clues hidden on
www.dragonbloodpirates.co.uk
To uncover them ye must enter a password,
that be the answer to the following question:

*What be the name of Jack and Al's
three-legged cat?*

Only one entry per child. Final draw 31 May 2011.
Runner-up draws will be held monthly until May 2011.
For full terms and conditions visit
www.dragonbloodpirates.co.uk/terms

www.dragonbloodpirates.co.uk

Ahoy there shipmates!

To reel in amazin' pirate booty, steer smartly
towards www.dragonbloodpirates.co.uk

Ye'll find games, downloads, activities and
sneak previews of the latest swashbucklin'
Dragon Blood Pirates adventures.
Learn how to speak all pirate-like, how to find
out what type of pirate ye be, an' what pirate
games ye can play with yer mates! This treasure
trove is a sure feast fer yer deadlights!

Only the bravest an' heartiest amon' ye
can become a true scurvy dog, so don't
ye miss a thing and sign up to yer newsletter
at www.dragonbloodpirates.co.uk!

Don't ye miss the other books in the
Dragon Blood Pirates
series!

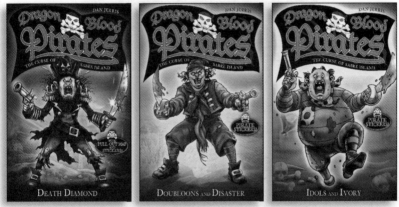

DEATH DIAMOND

978 1 40831 133 2

DOUBLOONS AND DISASTER

978 1 40830 739 7

IDOLS AND IVORY

978 1 40830 740 3

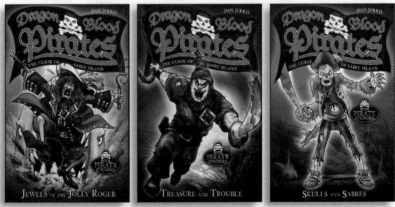

JEWELS OF THE JOLLY ROGER

978 1 40830 741 0

TREASURE AND TROUBLE

978 1 40830 742 7

SKULLS AND SABRES

978 1 40830 743 4

If you like

You'll love

Turn the page for
a gripping taste of

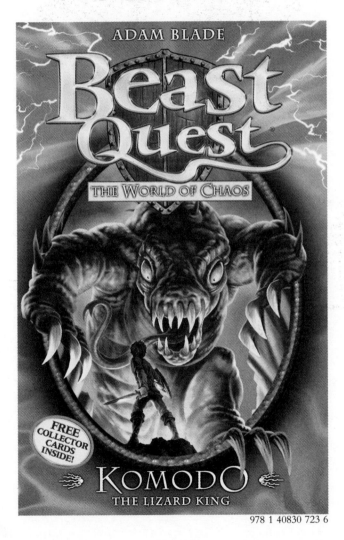

ADAM BLADE

Beast Quest

THE WORLD OF CHAOS

FREE COLLECTOR CARDS INSIDE!

KOMODO
THE LIZARD KING

978 1 40830 723 6

PROLOGUE

Badawi tugged up his scarf to cover
his nose and mouth, and pushed
headlong into a fresh storm that
swirled across Kayonia's freezing
desert. Grains of sand as cold as ice
stung his eyes. Around him the rest
of the tribe struggled onwards,
huddled in their furs. The column
of people and animals were tired
after a long day's march.

Every year they made this journey to reach warmer lands where they could barter their furs and precious metals at market, and each year the journey was just as hard.

Some say there are places where deserts are scorched with heat! Badawi thought.

He knew they would reach the end of the desert in another day or so, then the horses could graze in comfort.

If we ever make it...

The tribe's stocky horses, laden with heavy goods for trading, lumbered along, harnesses clinking. Badawi's horse was moving more slowly than the rest. The fungus infecting his hooves was growing worse by the day.

Two mares had already been lost on this journey and their loads had been shared among the other horses. The foot disease eventually made it impossible for the animals to walk. There was no choice but to leave the animals where they fell. Badawi knew that if more horses perished, the tribe would be stranded in the desert.

Only one thing was known to cure the disease – the Black Cactus.

If we don't find it soon, thought Badawi grimly, *we're in real trouble*.

Without horses, they couldn't trade; and if they couldn't trade, the tribe would starve.

As ever in Kayonia, night fell suddenly. Darkness descended like a black shroud, as two of the three moons rose into the sky. The wind dropped. Badawi pulled the scarf from his mouth and watched his breath form frozen clouds.

From the head of the group came the sound of shouting, and a murmur passed back along the line.

"We've found it!" called a voice.

Badawi led his horse out of the line and up to where Edwin, the leader of the tribe, was pointing. Silhouetted against the glowing orb of the third moon was a shape that everyone in the tribe recognised.

The Black Cactus.

It stood as tall as a man. The outer branches reached to the sky like grasping fingers, and hundreds of sharp spikes glittered in the moonlight. Badawi dismounted and ran across the sand as quickly as he could. It would only take a few drops of the Cactus juice to cure the horses' infection. The tribe was saved!

But his companions stopped. They
formed a semicircle, roughly twenty
paces from the Cactus. Badawi paused
beside them.

"What's the matter with you?"
he asked.

The men looked from one to the
other and finally Edwin spoke.

"You know what they say," said

the leader. "The Black Cactus is guarded by…"

"Nonsense!" said Badawi. "That's just a rumour to scare children."

Nobody moved.

"Fine," said Badawi. "If none of you has the courage to take a piece of the Cactus, it's up to me."

Still, as he walked towards the Cactus, his eyes searched the dark horizon, checking for attackers.

Nothing but sand. There's no monster here!

Badawi unsheathed his knife and knelt beside the Cactus. Its surface shone like ebony in the moonlight. Vicious spikes, each as long as his finger, but thin as a needle, jutted out. It was difficult to bring the knife close enough, but Badawi found a spot on one of the narrower branches. He used a sawing motion with his blade to cut into the flesh.

One of the tribe gasped. Before Badawi could turn, the sand beneath his knees seemed to lurch.

Badawi pitched forwards into the Cactus and the spikes tore open his sleeve, gouging his arm. He sucked air in through his teeth, trying not to cry out with pain.

The other tribesmen were backing away from him, looking on in fear. The ground shifted again under Badawi's feet, but this time he kept his balance. His eyes were fixed on the sand. Something pushed out from the swirling dune on the other side of the Cactus – a long, dark head with orange stripes running along a powerful jaw. Bulbous eyes swivelled onto Badawi as the rest of the body slithered out from the sand. Scaly black skin covered the Beast's hide and tail, crusted with orange warts. Its front claws and muscular hind legs thumped across the sand. A curved tongue darted from between its lips, tasting the air, hissing like red-hot metal plunged into water. Badawi's blood turned cold.

What they said was true. Komodo was real!

With a shake of its massive tail, the Beast charged at Badawi, who tripped backwards, dropping his knife. He heard shouts of terror from the rest of the tribe as they turned and ran.

Komodo stopped a few paces away from Badawi and reared up on his hindquarters, blotting out the moon. His throat inflated with a hiss and two flaps spread out like fans on either side of his face, flaring angry red.

Komodo's razor sharp front claws raked the air. Badawi cowered, too afraid to move. As the Beast lunged, the tribesman's screams ripped across the desert.

CHAPTER ONE
A NEW KINGDOM

Velmal stepped into the portal with Freya, preparing to depart the kingdom of Gwildor. Tom couldn't believe he had been reunited with his mother, only to have her snatched from him so soon. Freya cast a glance back at Tom before Velmal gave her an angry tug; the two of them were sucked down the swirling chute.

"No!" cried Tom, running towards

the coloured entrance to peer into the rainbow abyss. It was already beginning to shrink. He felt Elenna's hand on his shoulder, pulling him back.

"Are you sure about this?" she asked. "This portal could lead *anywhere*… You may never get home."

"I have to!" shouted Tom, as Storm and Silver gingerly inched over to them. "Freya's my mother…"

Elenna nodded. "Then we're coming, too."

Tom and Elenna turned to face the portal. "Ready?" he asked.

"Always," she replied.

Tom leapt into the magical tunnel, followed by his friends. The landscape melted away and Tom found his body flipping over in a powerful wind.

As he turned to look ahead, a flicker of purple caught Tom's eye: Velmal's robes. The evil Wizard was drifting some distance away. He held Freya's arm in a vice-like grip. Her black hair was snaking around her head and Velmal's robes buffeted against the tide of air.

"I have to rescue my mother," Tom shouted to Elenna. He dived onwards into the tunnel of light. Invisible forces smashed into his body, threatening to throw him against the sides of the chute, but Tom pulled himself through the air as though fighting a tempest at sea, straining his shoulders and arms to hold steady.